D1053109

The Not-So-Tiny Tales of

SiMON SEAHORSe

4

Summer School of Fish

By Cora Reef
Illustrated by Liam Darcy

LITTLE SIMON
New York   London   Toronto   Sydney   New Delhi

LITTLE SIMON
An imprint of Simon & Schuster Children's Publishing Division
1230 Avenue of the Americas, New York, New York 10020
First Little Simon hardcover edition May 2022
Copyright © 2022 by Simon & Schuster, Inc.
Also available in a Little Simon paperback edition.

The Simon & Schuster Speakers Bureau can bring authors to your live event. For more information or to book an event contact the Simon & Schuster Speakers Bureau at 1-866-248-3049 or visit our website at www.simonspeakers.com.
Designed by Leslie Mechanic
The text of this book was set in Causten Round.
Manufactured in the United States of America 0322 FFG
10 9 8 7 6 5 4 3 2 1
Library of Congress Cataloging-in-Publication Data
Names: Reef, Cora, author. | McDonald, Jake, illustrator.
Title: Summer school of fish / by Cora Reef ; illustrated by Jake McDonald.
Description: First Little Simon paperback edition. | New York : Little Simon, 2022. |
Series: The not-so-tiny tales of Simon Seahorse ; 4 | Audience: Ages 5-9. | Audience: Grades K-1. |
Summary: Simon and his best friend, Olive Octopus, attend summer camp together, but when Olive befriends Cam Crab, Simon questions if Olive is still his best friend. Identifiers: LCCN 2021044311 (print) | LCCN 2021044312 (ebook) | ISBN 9781665912105 (paperback) | ISBN 9781665912112 (hardcover) | ISBN 9781665912129 (ebook) Subjects: CYAC: Sea horses–Fiction. | Summer–Fiction. | Camps–Fiction. | Best friends–Fiction. | Friendship–Fiction. Classification: LCC PZ7.1.R4423 Su 2022 (print) | LCC PZ7.1.R4423 (ebook) | DDC [Fic]–dc23
LC record available at https://lccn.loc.gov/2021044311
LC ebook record available at https://lccn.loc.gov/2021044312

Contents

School's Out!

"And that's why the crystal jellyfish glows!" Simon Seahorse said.

The other students in the class cheered. Simon grinned as he swam back to his seat.

Simon had been excited to tell his classmates all about bioluminescent ocean creatures. He wished he could glow with electric light too! And he'd been extra excited about *this* report because it was the last one of the year.

"Nice job," his best friend, Olive Octopus, whispered as Simon sat down next to her.

"Thanks," Simon whispered back.

There was only one report to go. Then it would officially be Simon's favorite time of year: summer vacation. Simon loved school, but there was nothing like the freedom of summer.

"Thank you, Simon," Ms. Tuttle said. "Cam, it looks like you're our final presenter."

Simon squirmed in his seat as Cam Crab scuttled to the front of the room. Cam had a tendency to go a little overboard with his reports because he *really* loved facts. And he *really* loved showing everyone how much he knew about certain subjects.

"In my report I will be sharing dozens of fascinating facts about yeti crabs," Cam began.

Simon sighed and tried to pay attention. But Cam's report seemed even longer and duller than usual. Soon Simon's mind started to drift. He imagined the fun things he'd do this summer: sleep in late and eat lots of kelp ice cream and hang out with Olive and–

Simon's thoughts were suddenly interrupted by Cam's voice. "And that is my final fact about yeti crabs, just one of the many amazing crab species in the ocean." Then Cam took a bow and scurried back to his seat.

Simon clapped his fins in applause, relieved that the presentation was over.

"Thank you for your reports, everyone," Ms. Tuttle said. "And thank you for a wonderful year. I can't wait to see you again after summer break and hear about all the new and exciting things you did!"

The students started packing up their bags as Ms. Tuttle added, "Oh! And I will see a few of you in summer school very soon!"

Simon barely heard her. He was listening for the sound of the final school bell.

Brriing!

Everyone jumped out of their seats and started to swim outside.

"Come on, Olive!" Simon cried at the front of the crowd.

Olive laughed, grabbing her backpack. "I'm coming!"

The friends hurried out of the classroom and swam down toward the bottom level of the school. All the classes let out at the same time, so Simon watched as sea creatures of all ages hugged each other goodbye or chatted about summer plans.

Simon and Olive waved to their friends Nix and Lionel, who hopped into the current together. *They're probably headed to the Dunes,* Simon thought happily. Lionel loved sliding down the sand dunes.

Ah, summer. It's just the best!

The Summer of Trying New Things

As Simon waited for Olive to say good-bye to a blowfish from a different class, his mind once again began to wander.

He wanted to make sure they had the best summer ever. But how? Then he remembered something Ms. Tuttle had said. After Olive bid farewell to the blowfish, Simon told her his idea.

"Olive, what if we make this our 'summer of trying new things'?" Simon suggested.

Olive looked confused, so Simon went on. "Ms. Tuttle said she couldn't wait to hear about the new and exciting things we do this summer. So we could make sure we try as many new and exciting things as possible!"

Olive smiled. "I like that idea!" she said. Then she frowned. "As long as it doesn't involve bumping into any new *sharks*."

Simon laughed. One time, he and Olive had met a shark named Zelda. They were terrified of her at first, but she turned out to be really nice.

"I can't make any promises," said Simon. "What should we do first? Head to Seagrass Fields? The Coral Jungle? Sandy's Candy Shop? Oh, we can go check out the new slip-and-slide roller coaster at Coral Grove Water Park. I heard it's huge!"

Olive glanced at one of the many watches on her arms. "Sorry, Simon. I told my mom I'd help her get ready for the summer reading program at the library today."

Simon looked around to see if any other friends might want to join him on an adventure. But it seemed they were the last ones left at school.

"Okay," said Simon. "But we can do something new tomorrow, right?"

To his surprise, Olive laughed and said, "Yes, Simon. We can *definitely* do something new tomorrow." Then she hopped into the current that would bring her to the town library.

Simon floated in place for a moment, wondering if he should head to the water park on his own. But trying out the new roller coaster wouldn't be fun without Olive. So he finally sighed and headed home.

When he arrived at his house, Simon spotted a few of his siblings playing out front. The good thing about having eleven brothers and sisters was that even if you didn't have friends to play with, you had family!

Simon joined in a few rounds of hide-and-seek until his dad came home from the market.

Usually, Mr. Seahorse would ask them about homework. But today he said, "Happy last day of school!"

Everyone cheered.

"What did you get at the store, Dad?" Orion, one of Simon's older brothers, asked.

"Anything *new*?" Simon asked hopefully.

"Let's see," his dad said. "I got supplies for my famous kelp spaghetti, kelp chips, kelp waffles, and kelp burgers."

"Oh," Simon said. That all sounded good, but none of it was very new or exciting.

"And," Mr. Seahorse added, "I got a special treat to celebrate the end of the school year: kelp-berry shortcakes!"

"Hooray!" Simon cried. Then he followed his family inside to help their dad make dinner.

It was finally starting to feel like summer vacation!

What School?

As Simon piled kelp berries on top of his shortcake, he told his family about the plan he and Olive had come up with to try new things this summer.

"Olive said no new sharks. Zelda *could* show us new parts of Shark Point, though" he said. "And maybe we'll visit the hot springs in Misty Valley.

And of course, we *have* to try the new roller coaster at Coral Grove Water Park."

"That sounds like a great summer," said his oldest sister, Kya. She tossed up some kelp berries with her tail and then easily caught them in her mouth.

"I bet you'll have lots of exciting stories to tell," Earl chimed in. Simon's youngest brother loved hearing about Simon's adventures.

"Just remember, Simon," said Mr. Seahorse, "summer school starts tomorrow."

Simon blinked. "Summer school?"

"Yes, I told you about it last week,"
Mr. Seahorse said.

Simon thought back to last week.
He did remember his dad saying
something about taking classes

during the summer. But he'd been so focused on writing down one of his stories that he'd nodded without knowing what he was agreeing to.

"So I'll be in school *all* summer?" Simon asked.

"Only for the first few weeks," Mr. Seahorse said. Then he chuckled. "There's simply no way I can keep track of all twelve of you during the whole vacation. And luckily you're old enough for the program at the school now, Simon."

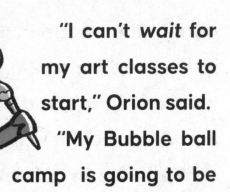

"I can't *wait* for my art classes to start," Orion said.

"My Bubble ball camp is going to be

so great this year," Kya said.

Simon's youngest sister, Lulu, began to pout. "I wish I were old enough to go

somewhere fun too!"

The others all started talking

over each other about the classes and camps they'd be doing during vacation. But Simon didn't join in. How was he supposed to try lots of new things this summer when he was stuck in school?

"Don't look so down, Simon," said his oldest brother, Jet. "It's not like going to regular school."

"Yeah," his older sister Izzy added. "It's really fun. And it just happens to be at the school. We all did it when we were your age."

Simon couldn't tell if his siblings were just trying to make him feel better. But he had to admit, he did feel a little better.

"Plus," Simon's dad said, "Olive will be there too."

"She will?" Simon asked. He suddenly felt relieved. If Olive were by his side, then summer school wouldn't be so bad.

Simon smiled. In fact, it could be a new thing they tried together!

First-Day Blues

The next morning, Simon was feeling a bit grumpy again. He was trying to be positive about summer school, but this was supposed to be summer *vacation*. And instead it felt like just another day of school. Simon ate his kelpflake cereal and packed up his backpack.

At least Olive will be there with me, he reminded himself. This had all probably been a surprise to her too. Or had it?

Suddenly Simon remembered the way Olive had laughed and said they'd *definitely* be doing something new the next day. Had she meant summer school?

Simon got to the corner of Seaweed Lane where Olive usually waited for him in the mornings, but she wasn't there. That was strange. Simon waited for a few minutes, but he didn't want to be late for his first day, so he jumped into the current alone and rode it toward Coral Grove Elementary.

Along the way, Simon spotted eels sunbathing, dolphins playing volleyball, and squid building sandcastles. He couldn't help feeling a little jealous as he watched them all enjoying their free time. *That* was what summer was supposed to be like.

When he finally got to the school, Simon didn't see any familiar faces. But he perked up when he spotted Ms. Tuttle greeting everyone.

"Hello, Simon," she said cheerfully. "It's nice to see you."

Simon smiled. At least Ms. Tuttle would be his teacher again.

"Your friends Olive and Cam are already in the art room," Ms. Tuttle went on. "That's where your pod will be meeting for summer school."

He was glad Olive was already there. But . . . Cam? Simon didn't dislike Cam exactly, but they didn't really see eye to eye. Simon loved to dream up fantastic stories. Cam wanted everything to be based on facts. Luckily, Olive usually took Simon's side when he and Cam disagreed.

Simon sped off to the art room to save Olive from Cam and his boring lists of facts. But when he got there, he was surprised to find Olive and Cam laughing together.

"Oh hi, Simon!" Olive said when he swam over to their table.

Cam stopped laughing and gave Simon a little nod hello.

"Did you know about this?" Simon asked Olive. "About summer school?"

Olive nodded. Then she smiled and said, "See, Cam? I told you Simon had no idea."

"I can't believe it!" Cam said. "Simon, how could you not know something this important?"

Suddenly Simon's face felt hot. "I just ... forgot," he mumbled.

"It's okay, Simon," Olive said. "I tried to forget too, but you know me ... I keep track of everything. And the good news is you made it on time!"

Simon nodded, but as he settled in beside Olive, he had an *un*settling feeling. Usually Simon and Olive were the ones laughing together, not Olive and . . . someone else.

Best Friends
Forever?

Summer school turned out to not be so bad after all. Like his siblings had said, it wasn't really like regular school. They had art and music and playground time—all of Simon's favorites.

In art, Ms. Tuttle said they could paint from a still life or paint from

their imagination. Simon eagerly got to work painting a fantastical scene full of pirates and mermaids and sea dragons. Olive and Cam both chose to do a still life.

"Wow, Cam," Olive said, studying his paper. "Your painting is so detailed."

Cam shrugged. "It's not perfect yet, but thanks."

In music, Ms. Tuttle asked for volunteers to play the seagrass harp. When Simon saw Olive raise one of her arms, he raised a fin too. But the teacher picked Olive and *Cam* instead. Simon ended up playing the conch shell tuba, which was fun too. But didn't Ms. Tuttle know that he and Olive always did things together?

When they got to the playground,
Simon immediately asked, "Want to
swim to the top of the sandcastle?"
It was his and Olive's favorite part of
the playground.

"No way," Cam said. "It's too high for me." Then he scuttled off toward the coral play structure instead.

"Looks like it's just us," Simon said to Olive. "Race you to the top?"

Olive hesitated. "How about we try the play structure with Cam today?"

"Really?" Simon said. "I thought you were worried about getting your arms wrapped around the bars."

"Well, I've never actually *tried* it," Olive said with a smile. "Maybe it'll be fun. And I feel bad that Cam is all on his own. Want to come?"

"Um, maybe later," Simon said. The truth was, he was too small for climbing the play structure. And he didn't want to embarrass himself. "You go ahead."

"Are you sure?" Olive asked.

Simon nodded.

As Olive followed Cam, Simon glanced around for someone else to play with. But he didn't know any of the other students very well. So finally he swam up to the top of the sandcastle alone. He watched as Cam and Olive played on the coral bars together down below.

When Simon thought about it, he wasn't surprised that Cam and Olive got along so well. They both loved facts and planning, and they paid attention to small details—much more than Simon did. Really, Olive probably had a lot more in common with Cam than she did with Simon.

Simon shook his head. All that didn't matter, right? They were best friends no matter what.

Weren't they?

Sandy's Candy Shop

When summer school let out for the day, Simon and Olive swam down to the bottom of the reef together.

"Do you want to go get some bubble chewies at Sandy's Candy Shop?" Simon asked Olive. "Maybe we can try some new flavors."

"Sure!" Olive said.

They noticed Cam nearby, scuttling along with his bulging backpack.

"Cam, do you want to come with us to get candy?" Olive asked.

Cam seemed surprised at the invitation, but he said, "Yes!"

Simon couldn't help but feel a little disappointed. He hadn't gotten to spend much time with Olive today. He'd been hoping they could finally plan out all the new things they *would* be able to do once summer school was over.

But at least he'd get to have some bubble chewies—the most delicious of candies.

"Hey, Olive," Simon said as they headed for the current, "do you remember that time I ate one hundred

and three bubble chewies in one day?"

"One hundred and three?" Cam said. "That's impossible!"

Olive laughed. "I don't know if it was exactly one hundred and three, but it was a lot."

When they arrived at Sandy's, Simon grabbed an extra-large bag for his candy, while Cam and Olive each took a smaller one.

KELP PINWHEEL SWIRLS

"What will it be today?" Sandy asked them. "Bubble chewies again?"

"Do you have any new flavors we could try?" Olive asked.

"Or new types of candy?" Simon added.

"Sure do!" Sandy said. Then she loaded up their bags with all sorts of treats they'd never had before.

Simon noticed that Cam was off on
his own, filling up his entire bag with
gold-foil kelp rolls.

"Don't you want to
try something new?"
Simon asked Cam
when they'd finished
filling their bags.

Cam shook his head. "Kelp rolls are my favorite. Why change a good thing?"

"Because you could be missing out on something even better," Simon pointed out. "One time, I tried a  kelp pop that was a mystery flavor, and it turned out . . . well, it turned out to be sand-flavored, but that's not the point."

Cam shrugged. "I know what I like," he said, and twisted the top of his bag into a knot. Then he scuttled out.

"Cam sure is one crabby crab sometimes," Simon said to Olive with a nudge.

Olive smiled but didn't respond. The she too swam outside.

All
Alone

That evening at dinner, Simon told his family all about what he'd done at summer school.

"I'm glad to hear you had a good first day!" Mr. Seahorse said, smiling.

Simon smiled back, but his stomach squeezed tight. Today *had* been good, and yet . . . he couldn't stop thinking about Olive and Cam being buddies.

It had always been Simon and Olive. They'd been best friends ever since he could remember. When his stories went over the top, Olive brought him back to reality. When Olive needed some encouragement to be more adventurous, Simon was

there for her. They always counted on each other. But could they still?

Simon tried to put the thought out of his mind as he got into bed that night. He'd meet Olive at the corner of Seaweed Lane tomorrow and they'd ride the current to school together, as always. Then things would be back to normal.

But in the morning, Simon waited and waited at the corner of Seaweed Lane. Olive didn't come. Finally, Simon hopped into the current alone.

Simon arrived at school to find Olive heading toward the classroom with Cam.

"Olive, where were you this morning?" Simon asked. "I thought we were meeting at the corner, like always."

"Oh, I stopped by the library with my mom first," Olive said. "Just like I did yesterday."

"Oh," said Simon, realizing she was right. They hadn't ridden the current together yesterday either. But still ...

"All right, let's get started," Ms. Tuttle said. "We have some fun new art projects today."

"Ooh, something new," Olive said, looking at Simon.

Simon smiled back. So Olive was still thinking about their "summer of trying new things"! But then Olive went to sit with Cam again, and Simon's smile faded.

All morning, he watched as Olive and Cam did pretty much everything together.

"Simon, do you want to have lunch with us at the picnic tables?" Olive asked after art time. "Cam's going to tell me some funny facts about hermit crabs."

"Uh, that's okay," Simon said. He did *not* want to sit through another one of Cam's reports. "I need to go ask Ms. Tuttle about something," he added. Then he swam back inside and ate in the classroom by himself.

After lunch, Simon worked on his own again. He decided to try out the water balloon art project. Olive had said she worried it would be too messy. At playground time, Simon went to check out the sandcastle tower, which was the tallest thing on the playground. He'd never been inside before because Olive couldn't fit through the tiny window.

The view from the top of the tower was even better than he'd imagined. Simon only wished Olive were there to enjoy it with him.

The Big
Race

The rest of summer school went by pretty much the same way. Simon kept mostly to himself while Olive and Cam seemed to always be having a great time together.

It wasn't that Olive was ignoring Simon. She always invited him to do whatever she and Cam were doing.

But Simon didn't know where he fit in.

Finally, it was the last day of summer school. Simon arrived alone, as usual.

"Hi, Simon!" a lionfish named Polly called out. Simon had eaten lunch with her and her friends a few times. "Looks like you're all ready for the big relay race today."

"I sure am!" Simon told her. Despite how down he was feeling about things with Olive, he was excited about the race. He'd even worn his bubble ball gear to school.

"Okay, everyone," Ms. Tuttle said once they were out on the field. "You'll be split into two teams for the relay race: the blue team and the red team." She started going through her list and putting the students onto teams.

Cam and Olive cheered when they found out they'd both be on the red team.

Simon held his breath when Ms. Tuttle came to him. "Simon Seahorse, you're on the red team too," she said.

"Oh good, Simon, you're with us!" said Olive when he swam over to join them.

"And now, everyone, please find a partner!" Ms. Tuttle called out.

Simon, Olive, and Cam all looked at each other. Simon's heart sank.

Before anyone could say anything, Simon blurted out, "Olive, Cam, you two can pair up. I'll find someone else." Then he swam off, relieved to have avoided an awkward moment.

"Simon, do you want to be with me?" Polly asked, waving him over.

Simon nodded. "Sure. Thanks."

He and Polly turned out to be a good team. The relay race involved a few different levels. Even though

Simon was small, playing bubble ball had taught him to be fast. And Polly's long fins helped propel her through the water.

Together, they came in before most of their team.

When everyone had finished, Ms. Tuttle tallied how many pairs on each team had won. Finally, she announced the winner. "Our summer school relay race winner is the blue team!"

As the blue team cheered and huddled up, Simon swam over to his teammates from the red team.

He sighed. His team had lost, but *that* wasn't why he felt so down.

Taking
a Chance

After Ms. Tuttle had handed out seashell trophies to *all* the students, Simon took his and headed for the current. But Olive caught up to him.

"Simon! Where are you going?" she asked.

"Oh, I'm heading home," Simon said. "My dad's making a big dinner

to celebrate the end of summer school."

"Yum!" Olive said with a smile. But then her smile faded. "Hey ... why didn't you want to be my partner for the race?" she asked.

Simon looked at her in surprise. "I figured you'd want to partner with Cam," he replied. "You two are so close now. You're ... well, you're best friends."

Olive smiled bigger now. "Oh, Simon! I really like Cam, and we do have a lot in common. But you'll always be my best friend."

"But . . . but you've been spending *so* much time with Cam this summer," Simon added.

"Well, you seemed to want to be alone," Olive said. "I thought maybe it was part of your plan to try new things. You know, since we usually do so much together. The other day I saw that you went into the sandcastle tower. You know I can't fit into that. How was it?"

Simon blinked. He *had* said he wanted to try new things this summer.

"Plus I thought it might be nice if I got to know Cam better—as something else new," Olive continued. "And you know what? I'm glad I did that. Cam *can* be a little crabby sometimes. But he's also really nice—and funny."

"Funny?" Simon said in disbelief.

Olive smiled. "In his own way."

Just then Cam scuttled over. "Good race, Simon," he said.

"Thanks! You too," Simon said, suddenly feeling a lot more cheerful.

"I have an idea," Olive said to the two of them. "Now that summer school's over, how about we all go to the Coral Grove Water Park together tomorrow?"

"Yes!" Simon cried. "Finally we can try out the new roller coaster!"

Cam's eyes widened. "Roller coaster? That sounds ... scary."

"It might be!" Simon said. "But we can try it together."

Cam nodded. "I guess I could give it a chance," he said.

"It's always nice to try something new," Olive added, smiling at Simon. "We can meet at the corner of Seaweed Lane tomorrow and take the current together."

"Make sure to pack extra snacks," said Simon. "Olive, remember last time we went to the water park, my kelp-and-butter crackers fell out of my bag and flew right into the mouth of the lobster behind me? Luckily, my friend Walter the orca saw what happened and offered me a whale-size snack instead!"

Olive laughed. "Well, I remember *some* of that," she said.

"Yeah." Simon laughed. "The Walter part *may* have happened in my imagination," he admitted. "But doesn't it make for a good story?"

He was surprised when Cam nodded and said, "Yes, actually, it does."

3-2-1–
GO!

The next morning, the three friends met at the corner of Seaweed Lane.

"Did everyone bring extra snacks?" Simon asked.

Cam held up the bag of kelp rolls from Sandy's Candy Shop. It was still almost full. Simon couldn't believe it. He'd eaten *his* candy ages ago.

As they hopped onto the current, they shared the snacks they'd brought. Simon was surprised at how much he liked kelp rolls. He hadn't had them in so long, he'd forgotten that they were really tasty. No wonder they were Cam's favorite.

Soon enough, they arrived at the water park. The trio stood at the entrance with their mouths hanging

open. Past the Sea Snake Rapids, the Wacky Water Slide, and the Fizzing Fountains stood the brand-new Colossal Slip-and-Slide Coaster.

"It's so big," said Olive.

"It's so high," said Cam.

"It's so *awesome!*" Simon cried.

"Why don't we ease our way in and start with the rapids," Olive suggested.

"Good idea," Cam said.

They hopped onto a boat together and giggled as they went over huge rapids that practically threw them overboard! Luckily they were all expert swimmers.

After that, they splashed through the Fizzing Fountains and zipped down the Wacky Water Slide.

As they got closer to the roller coaster, Simon could see just how big it really was.

"Should we go up?" Olive asked when they'd done all the other rides.

Simon gulped. "Um, it's getting late. Maybe we should wait until next time."

Cam frowned. "What happened to trying new things?" he asked.

"Well . . . ," Simon began.

"Well," Cam said, "we can't leave without trying the *newest* ride, can we?"

"Really, Cam? *You* want to go on *that*?" said Olive.

To Simon's surprise, Cam smiled and said, "It turns out I like rides. Who knew?"

"What do you think, Simon?" Olive asked. "Should we give the roller coaster a try?"

Simon glanced up at the giant, looping coaster. Then he looked back at Olive and Cam. Suddenly the coaster didn't seem quite so scary. As long as his friends were by his side, he knew he'd be all right.

"Let's do it," he said.

The three of them swam to the top of the coaster. They waited in line for their turn.

"Ready?" Olive asked when they were all buckled in.

"Ready!" Simon and Cam said together.

"Three-two-one...GO!" Olive cried.

The three friends pushed off together and zoomed along the giant slip-and-slide coaster, laughing all the way down.

SIMON'S STORY

Sly Seahorse and Orla Octopus were best friends. They did everything together, like brother and sister. But without the sibling fighting. One time, Sly saved Orla from a group of piranhas! Another time, Orla guided them home from Shark Point! But

then Charlie Crab came along, and Orla started spending all her time with Charlie. Sly felt pretty sad. He didn't have his pal when an anglerfish almost ate him! He didn't have her when he got lost near Kelp Forest. But when he and Orla finally talked about it, she said they'd always be best friends. And Sly knew that was true. They truly were meant to be best friends forever— and now they had a new friend too!

THE END

Here's a peek at Simon's next big adventure!

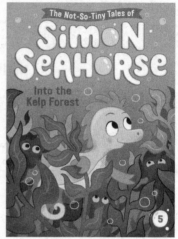

"Race you to the top of the sandcastle!" Simon Seahorse cried.

He was talking to his best friend, Olive Octopus. The sandcastle on the school playground was their favorite place to hang out during recess.

An excerpt from *Into the Kelp Forest*

But as Simon and Olive got ready to race, something caught Simon's eye. It was his eel friend, Nix. She was over by the seaweed swings with a small crowd of their classmates. She was talking in a loud voice and making grand gestures with her long tail.

"Hey, what's going on over there?" Simon asked.

Olive glanced over. "Let's go see!" she said.

When Simon and Olive swam closer, they realized Nix was telling a story. The others were listening with wide eyes.

An excerpt from *Into the Kelp Forest*

"And they say," Nix whispered, "that the Kelp Monster has been haunting the Kelp Forest ever since."

There was a long, spooky silence.

"Is that true?" a young parrotfish finally asked.

"Oh yes," Lionel, Simon's clownfish classmate, jumped in. "I heard about the monster from my sister. She said its teeth are sharper than a red-bellied piranha's."

"I heard it's bigger than a whale shark!" cried a lobster from another class.

An excerpt from *Into the Kelp Forest*